TALKING IS NOT MY THING!

A book to share from

Scallywag Press

For Rowland

ACKNOWLEDGEMENTS

I owe an extraordinary debt to the people whom I have
approached for guidance whilst writing this book:
Lilo, Frances and Carly.

In particular, I would like to thank Dr Rebecca Butler for her
continual advice and support throughout the production
of this book. **R.R.**

First published in Great Britain in 2020 by Scallywag Press Ltd,
10 Sutherland Row, London SW1V 4JT.

This paperback edition published in 2021

Copyright © 2020 by Rose Robbins

The rights of Rose Robbins to be identified as the author and illustrator of this work have been asserted by her
in accordance with the Copyright, Designs and Patents Act, 1988.

All rights reserved.

Art Direction and design by Sarah Finan

Printed in Malaysia by Tien Wah Press

001

British Library Cataloguing in Publication Data available.

ISBN 978-1-912650-59-0

TALKING IS NOT MY THING!

ROSE ROBBINS

Scallywag Press Ltd
LONDON

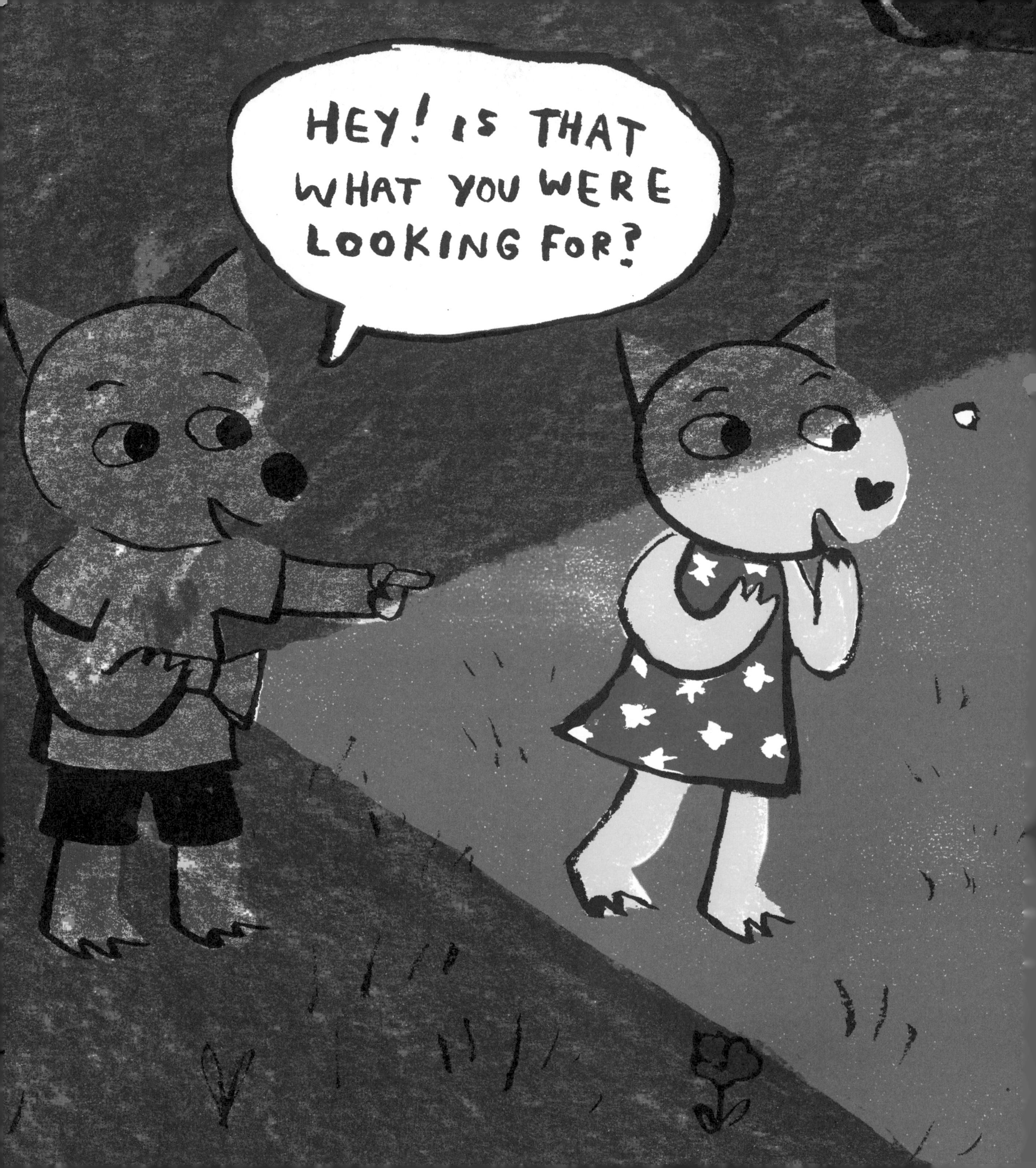
HEY! IS THAT WHAT YOU WERE LOOKING FOR?

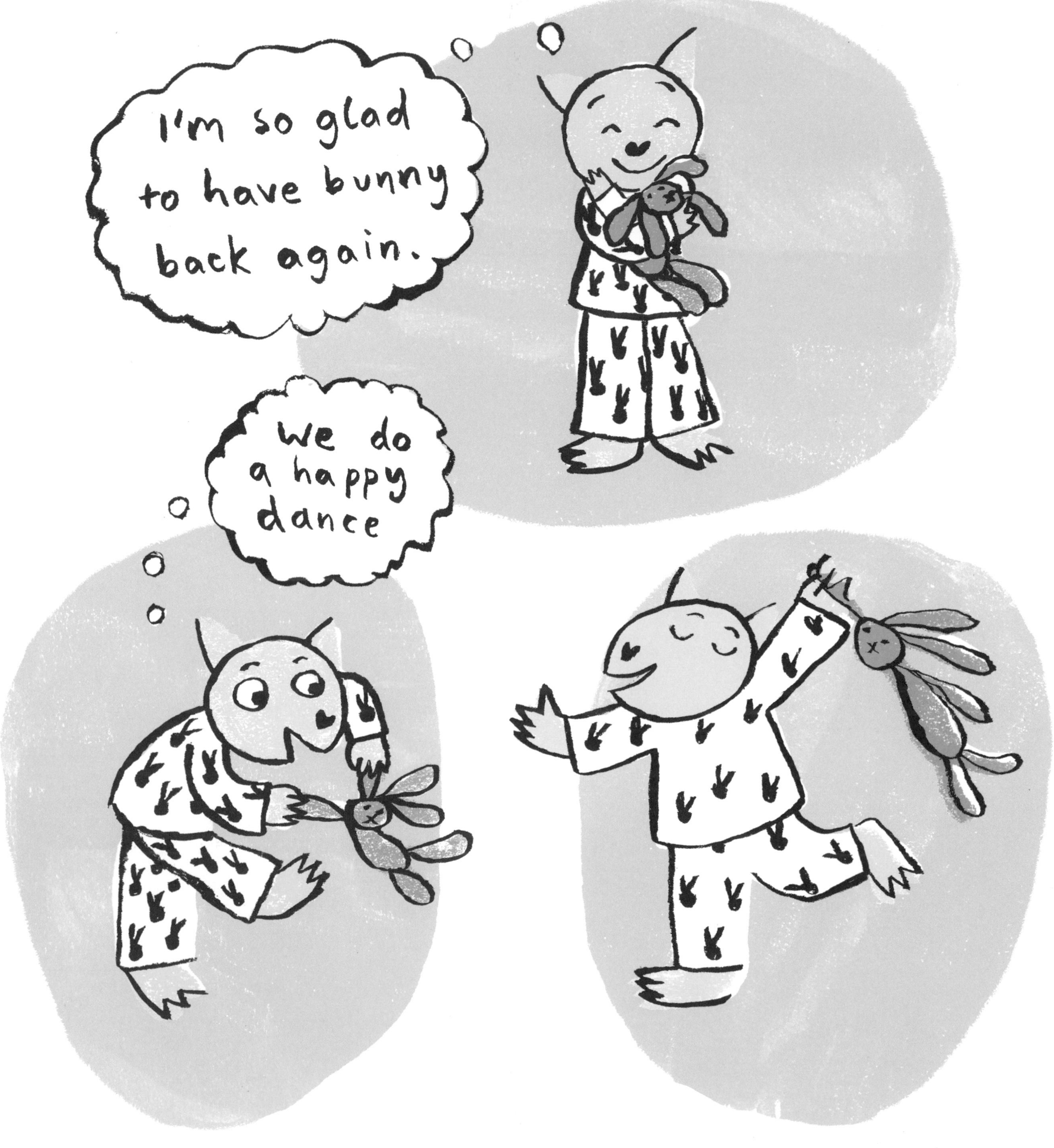
I'm so glad to have bunny back again.
We do a happy dance